ARARAT

BY

Louise Glück

THE ECCO PRESS

The Ecco Press
100 West Broad Street
Hopewell, NJ 08525
Published simultaneously in Canada by
Penguin Books Canada Ltd., Ontario
Printed in the United States of America

Design and composition by
The Sarabande Press

The author wishes to acknowledge the editor of *Ironwood,* in which
"Lullaby," "Birthday," "Snow," and "Celestial Music" have appeared.
Special thanks to the Guggenheim Foundation and the National
Endowment for the Arts for their support.

Library of Congress Cataloging-in-Publication Data

Glück, Louise, 1943–
Ararat / by Louise Glück.—1st pbk. ed.
p.   cm.—(American poetry series)
$9.95
I. Title. II. Series: American poetry series (Unnumbered)
[PS3557.L8A89   1992]   811'.54—dc20   91-36417 CIP
ISBN 0-88001-248-X

The text of this book is set in Janson.

9 8 7 6 5 4 3

CONTENTS

"... *human nature was originally one and we were a whole, and the desire and pursuit of the whole is called love.*"

—*Plato*

ARARAT

PARODOS

Long ago, I was wounded.
I learned
to exist, in reaction,
out of touch
with the world: I'll tell you
what I meant to be—
a device that listened.
Not inert: still.
A piece of wood. A stone.

Why should I tire myself, debating, arguing?
Those people breathing in the other beds
could hardly follow, being
uncontrollable
like any dream—
Through the blinds, I watched
the moon in the night sky, shrinking and swelling—

I was born to a vocation:
to bear witness
to the great mysteries.
Now that I've seen both
birth and death, I know
to the dark nature these
are proofs, not
mysteries—

A FANTASY

I'll tell you something: every day
people are dying. And that's just the beginning.
Every day, in funeral homes, new widows are born,
new orphans. They sit with their hands folded,
trying to decide about this new life.

Then they're in the cemetery, some of them
for the first time. They're frightened of crying,
sometimes of not crying. Someone leans over,
tells them what to do next, which might mean
saying a few words, sometimes
throwing dirt in the open grave.

And after that, everyone goes back to the house,
which is suddenly full of visitors.
The widow sits on the couch, very stately,
so people line up to approach her,
sometimes take her hand, sometimes embrace her.
She finds something to say to everybody,
thanks them, thanks them for coming.

In her heart, she wants them to go away.
She wants to be back in the cemetery,
back in the sickroom, the hospital. She knows

it isn't possible. But it's her only hope,
the wish to move backward. And just a little,
not so far as the marriage, the first kiss.

A NOVEL

No one could write a novel about this family:
too many similar characters. Besides, they're all women;
there was only one hero.

Now the hero's dead. Like echoes, the women last longer;
they're all too tough for their own good.

From this point on, nothing changes:
there's no plot without a hero.
In this house, when you say *plot* what you mean is *love story*.

The women can't get moving.
Oh, they get dressed, they eat, they keep up appearances.
But there's no action, no development of character.

They're all determined to suppress
criticism of the hero. The problem is
he's weak; his scenes specify
his function but not his nature.

Maybe that explains why his death wasn't moving.
First he's sitting at the head of the table,
where the figurehead is most needed.
Then he's dying, a few feet away, his wife holding a mirror
    under his mouth.

Amazing, how they keep busy, these women, the wife and two
     daughters.
Setting the table, clearing the dishes away.
Each heart pierced through with a sword.

LABOR DAY

It's a year exactly since my father died.
Last year was hot. At the funeral, people talked about the
  weather.
How hot it was for September. How unseasonable.

This year, it's cold.
There's just us now, the immediate family.
In the flower beds,
shreds of bronze, of copper.

Out front, my sister's daughter rides her bicycle
the way she did last year,
up and down the sidewalk. What she wants is
to make time pass.

While to the rest of us
a whole lifetime is nothing.
One day, you're a blond boy with a tooth missing;
the next, an old man gasping for air.
It comes to nothing, really, hardly
a moment on earth.
Not a sentence, but a breath, a caesura.

LOVER OF FLOWERS

In our family, everyone loves flowers.
That's why the graves are so odd:
no flowers, just padlocks of grass,
and in the center, plaques of granite,
the inscriptions terse, the shallow letters
sometimes filling with dirt.
To clean them out, you use your handkerchief.

With my sister, it's different,
it's an obsession. Weekends, she sits on my mother's porch,
reading catalogues. Every autumn, she plants bulbs by the
     brick stoop;
every spring, waits for flowers.
No one discusses cost. It's understood
my mother pays; after all,
it's her garden, every flower
planted for my father. They both see
the house as his true grave.

Not everything thrives on Long Island.
Sometimes the summer gets too hot;
sometimes a heavy rain beats down the flowers.
That's how the poppies died, after one day,
because they're very fragile.

My mother's tense, upset about my sister:

now she'll never know how beautiful they were,
pure pink, with no dark spots. That means
she's going to feel deprived again.

But for my sister, that's the condition of love.
She was my father's daughter:
the face of love, to her,
is the face turning away.

WIDOWS

My mother's playing cards with my aunt,
Spite and Malice, the family pastime, the game
my grandmother taught all her daughters.

Midsummer: too hot to go out.
Today, my aunt's ahead; she's getting the good cards.
My mother's dragging, having trouble with her concentration.
She can't get used to her own bed this summer.
She had no trouble last summer,
getting used to the floor. She learned to sleep there
to be near my father.
He was dying; he got a special bed.

My aunt doesn't give an inch, doesn't make
allowance for my mother's weariness.
It's how they were raised: you show respect by fighting.
To let up insults the opponent.

Each player has one pile to the left, five cards in the hand.
It's good to stay inside on days like this,
to stay where it's cool.
And this is better than other games, better than solitaire.

My grandmother thought ahead; she prepared her daughters.
They have cards; they have each other.
They don't need any more companionship.

All afternoon the game goes on but the sun doesn't move.
It just keeps beating down, turning the grass yellow.
That's how it must seem to my mother.
And then, suddenly, something is over.

My aunt's been at it longer; maybe that's why she's playing
    better.
Her cards evaporate: that's what you want, that's the object: in
    the end,
the one who has nothing wins.

CONFESSION

To say I'm without fear—
it wouldn't be true.
I'm afraid of sickness, humiliation.
Like anyone, I have my dreams.
But I've learned to hide them,
to protect myself
from fulfillment: all happiness
attracts the Fates' anger.
They are sisters, savages—
in the end, they have
no emotion but envy.

A PRECEDENT

In the same way as she'd prepare for the others,
my mother planned for the child that died.

Bureaus of soft clothes.
Little jackets neatly folded.
Each one almost fit in the palm of a hand.

In the same way, she wondered
which day would be its birthday.
And as each passed, she knew a day as common
would become a symbol of joy.

Because death hadn't touched my mother's life,
she was thinking of something else,
dreaming, the way you do when a child's coming.

LOST LOVE

My sister spent a whole life in the earth.
She was born, she died.
In between,
not one alert look, not one sentence.

She did what babies do,
she cried. But she didn't want to be fed.
Still, my mother held her, trying to change
first fate, then history.

Something did change: when my sister died,
my mother's heart became
very cold, very rigid,
like a tiny pendant of iron.

Then it seemed to me my sister's body
was a magnet. I could feel it draw
my mother's heart into the earth,
so it would grow.

LULLABY

My mother's an expert in one thing:
sending people she loves into the other world.
The little ones, the babies—these
she rocks, whispering or singing quietly. I can't say
what she did for my father;
whatever it was, I'm sure it was right.

It's the same thing, really, preparing a person
for sleep, for death. The lullabies—they all say
don't be afraid, that's how they paraphrase
the heartbeat of the mother.
So the living slowly grow calm; it's only
the dying who can't, who refuse.

The dying are like tops, like gyroscopes—
they spin so rapidly they seem to be still.
Then they fly apart: in my mother's arms,
my sister was a cloud of atoms, of particles—that's the
    difference.
When a child's asleep, it's still whole.

My mother's seen death; she doesn't talk about the soul's
    integrity.
She's held an infant, an old man, as by comparison the dark
    grew
solid around them, finally changing to earth.

The soul's like all matter:
why would it stay intact, stay faithful to its one form,
when it could be free?

MOUNT ARARAT

Nothing's sadder than my sister's grave
unless it's the grave of my cousin, next to her.
To this day, I can't bring myself to watch
my aunt and my mother,
though the more I try to escape
seeing their suffering, the more it seems
the fate of our family:
each branch donates one girl child to the earth.

In my generation, we put off marrying, put off having
    children.
When we did have them, we each had one;
for the most part, we had sons, not daughters.

We don't discuss this ever.
But it's always a relief to bury an adult,
someone remote, like my father.
It's a sign that maybe the debt's finally been paid.

In fact, no one believes this.
Like the earth itself, every stone here
is dedicated to the Jewish god
who doesn't hesitate to take
a son from a mother.

APPEARANCES

When we were children, my parents had our portraits painted,
then hung them side by side, over the mantel,
where we couldn't fight.
I'm the dark one, the older one. My sister's blond,
the one who looks angry because she can't talk.

It never bothered me, not talking.
That hasn't changed much. My sister's still blond, not different
from the portrait. Except we're adults now, we've been
    analyzed:
we understand our expressions.

My mother tried to love us equally,
dressed us in the same dresses; she wanted us
perceived as sisters.
That's what she wanted from the portraits:
you need to see them hanging together, facing one another—
separated, they don't make the same statement.
You wouldn't know what the eyes were fixed on;
they'd seem to be staring into space.

This was the summer we went to Paris, the summer I was
    seven.
Every morning, we went to the convent.
Every afternoon, we sat still, having the portraits painted,

wearing green cotton dresses, the square neck marked with a
    ruffle.
Monsieur Davanzo added the flesh tones: my sister's ruddy;
    mine, faintly bluish.
To amuse us, Madame Davanzo hung cherries over our ears.

It was something I was good at: sitting still, not moving.
I did it to be good, to please my mother, to distract her from
    the child that died.
I wanted to be child enough. I'm still the same,
like a toy that can stop and go, but not change direction.

Anyone can love a dead child, love an absence.
My mother's strong; she doesn't do what's easy.
She's like her mother: she believes in family, in order.
She doesn't change her house, just freshens the paint
    occasionally.
Sometimes something breaks, gets thrown away, but that's all.
She likes to sit there, on the blue couch, looking up at her
    daughters,
at the two who lived. She can't remember how it really was,
how anytime she ministered to one child, loved that child,
she damaged the other. You could say
she's like an artist with a dream, a vision.
Without that, she'd have been torn apart.

We were like the portraits, always together: you had to shut out
one child to see the other.
That's why only the painter noticed: a face already so
        controlled, so withdrawn,
and too obedient, the clear eyes saying
If you want me to be a nun, I'll be a nun.

THE UNTRUSTWORTHY SPEAKER

Don't listen to me; my heart's been broken.
I don't see anything objectively.

I know myself; I've learned to hear like a psychiatrist.
When I speak passionately,
that's when I'm least to be trusted.

It's very sad, really: all my life, I've been praised
for my intelligence, my powers of language, of insight.
In the end, they're wasted—

I never see myself,
standing on the front steps, holding my sister's hand.
That's why I can't account
for the bruises on her arm, where the sleeve ends.

In my own mind, I'm invisible: that's why I'm dangerous.
People like me, who seem selfless,
we're the cripples, the liars;
we're the ones who should be factored out
in the interest of truth.

When I'm quiet, that's when the truth emerges.
A clear sky, the clouds like white fibers.
Underneath, a little gray house, the azaleas
red and bright pink.

If you want the truth, you have to close yourself
to the older daughter, block her out:
when a living thing is hurt like that,
in its deepest workings,
all function is altered.

That's why I'm not to be trusted.
Because a wound to the heart
is also a wound to the mind.

A FABLE

Two women with
the same claim
came to the feet of
the wise king. Two women,
but only one baby.
The king knew
someone was lying.
What he said was
Let the child be
cut in half; that way
no one will go
empty-handed. He
drew his sword.
Then, of the two
women, one
renounced her share:
this was
the sign, the lesson.
Suppose
you saw your mother
torn between two daughters:
what could you do
to save her but be
willing to destroy
yourself—she would know
who was the rightful child,

the one who couldn't bear
to divide the mother.

NEW WORLD

As I saw it,
all my mother's life, my father
held her down, like
lead strapped to her ankles.

She was
buoyant by nature;
she wanted to travel,
go to theater, go to museums.
What he wanted
was to lie on the couch
with the *Times*
over his face,
so that death, when it came,
wouldn't seem a significant change.

In couples like this,
where the agreement
is to do things together,
it's always the active one
who concedes, who gives.
You can't go to museums
with someone who won't
open his eyes.

I thought my father's death
would free my mother.
In a sense, it has:
she takes trips, looks at
great art. But she's floating.
Like some child's balloon
that gets lost the minute
it isn't held.
Or like an astronaut
who somehow loses the ship
and has to drift in space
knowing, however long it lasts,
this is what's left of being alive: she's free
in that sense.
Without relation to earth.

BIRTHDAY

Every year, on her birthday, my mother got twelve roses
from an old admirer. Even after he died, the roses kept
    coming:
the way some people leave paintings and furniture,
this man left bulletins of flowers,
his way of saying that the legend of my mother's beauty
had simply gone underground.

At first, it seemed bizarre.
Then we got used to it: every December, the house suddenly
filling with flowers. They even came to set
a standard of courtesy, of generosity—

After ten years, the roses stopped.
But all that time I thought
the dead could minister to the living;
I didn't realize
this was the anomaly; that for the most part
the dead were like my father.

My mother doesn't mind, she doesn't need
displays from my father.
Her birthday comes and goes; she spends it
sitting by a grave.

She's showing him she understands,
that she accepts his silence.
He hates deception: she doesn't want him making
signs of affection when he can't feel.

BROWN CIRCLE

My mother wants to know
why, if I hate
family so much,
I went ahead and
had one. I don't
answer my mother.
What I hated
was being a child,
having no choice about
what people I loved.

I don't love my son
the way I meant to love him.
I thought I'd be
the lover of orchids who finds
red trillium growing
in the pine shade, and doesn't
touch it, doesn't need
to possess it. What I am
is the scientist,
who comes to that flower
with a magnifying glass
and doesn't leave, though
the sun burns a brown
circle of grass around
the flower. Which is

more or less the way
my mother loved me.

I must learn
to forgive my mother,
now that I'm helpless
to spare my son.

CHILDREN COMING HOME FROM SCHOOL

1.

If you live in a city, it's different: someone has to meet
the child at the bus stop. There's a reason. A child all alone
can disappear, get lost, maybe forever.

My sister's daughter wants to walk home alone; she thinks she's
        old enough.
My sister thinks it's too soon for such a big change;
the best her daughter gets
is the option to walk without holding hands.

That's what they do; they compromise, which anyone
can manage for a few blocks. My niece gets one hand
totally free; my sister says
if she's old enough to walk this way, she's old enough
to hold her own violin.

2.

My son accuses me
of his unhappiness, not
in words, but in the way
he stares at the ground, inching
slowly up the driveway: he knows
I'm watching. That's why
he greets the cat,

to show he's capable
of open affection.
My father used
the dog in the same way.
My son and I, we're the living
experts in silence.
Snow's sweeping the sky;
it shifts directions, going
first steadily down, then sideways.

3.

One thing you learn, growing up with my sister:
you learn that rules don't mean anything.
Sooner or later, whatever you're waiting to hear will get itself
    said.
It doesn't matter what it is: *I love you* or *I'll never speak to you*
    again.
It all gets said, often in the same night.

Then you slip in, you take advantage. There are ways
to hold a person to what's been said; for example, by using the
    word *promise.*
But you have to have patience; you have to be able to wait, to
    listen.

My niece knows that in time, with intelligence, she'll get
    everything she wants.
It's not a bad life. Of course, she has those gifts,
time and intelligence.

ANIMALS

My sister and I reached
the same conclusion:
the best way
to love us was to not
spend time with us.
It seemed that
we appealed
chiefly to strangers.
We had good clothes, good
manners in public.

In private, we were
always fighting. Usually
the big one finished
sitting on the little one
and pinching her.
The little one
bit: in forty years
she never learned
the advantage in not
leaving a mark.

The parents
had a credo: they didn't
believe in anger.
The truth was, for different reasons,

they couldn't bring themselves
to inflict pain. You should only hurt
something you can give
your whole heart to. They preferred
tribunals: the child
most in the wrong could choose
her own punishment.

My sister and I
never became allies,
never turned on our parents.
We had
other obsessions: for example,
we both felt there were
too many of us
to survive.

We were like animals
trying to share a dry pasture.
Between us, one tree, barely
strong enough to sustain
a single life.

We never moved
our eyes from each other
nor did either touch
one thing that could
feed her sister.

SAINTS

In our family, there were two saints,
my aunt and my grandmother.
But their lives were different.

My grandmother's was tranquil, even at the end.
She was like a person walking in calm water;
for some reason
the sea couldn't bring itself to hurt her.
When my aunt took the same path,
the waves broke over her, they attacked her,
which is how the Fates respond
to a true spiritual nature.

My grandmother was cautious, conservative:
that's why she escaped suffering.
My aunt's escaped nothing;
each time the sea retreats, someone she loves is taken away.

Still, she won't experience
the sea as evil. To her, it is what it is:
where it touches land, it must turn to violence.

YELLOW DAHLIA

My sister's like a sun, like a yellow dahlia.
Daggers of gold hair around the face.
Gray eyes, full of spirit.

I made an enemy of a flower:
now, I'm ashamed.

We were supposed to be opposites:
one fair, like daylight.
One different, negative.

If there are two things
then one must be better,
isn't that true? I know now
we both thought that, if what children do
can really be called thinking.

I look at my sister's daughter,
a child so like her,
and I'm ashamed: nothing justifies
the impulse to destroy
a smaller, a dependent life.

I guess I knew that always.
That's why I had to hurt
myself instead:

I believed in justice.

We were like day and night,
one act of creation.
I couldn't separate
the two halves,
one child from the other.

COUSINS

My son's very graceful; he has perfect balance.
He's not competitive, like my sister's daughter.

Day and night, she's always practicing.
Today, it's hitting softballs into the copper beech,
retrieving them, hitting them again.
After a while, no one even watches her.
If she were any stronger, the tree would be bald.

My son won't play with her; he won't even ride bicycles with
      her.
She accepts that; she's used to playing by herself.
The way she sees it, it isn't personal:
whoever won't play doesn't like losing.

It's not that my son's inept, that he doesn't do things well.
I've watched him race: he's natural, effortless —
right from the first, he takes the lead.
And then he stops. It's as though he was born rejecting
the solitude of the victor.

My sister's daughter doesn't have that problem.
She may as well be first; she's already alone.

PARADISE

I grew up in a village: now
it's almost a city.
People came from the city, wanting
something simple, something
better for the children.
Clean air; nearby
a little stable.
All the streets
named after sweethearts or girl children.

Our house was gray, the sort of place
you buy to raise a family.
My mother's still there, all alone.
When she's lonely, she watches television.

The houses get closer together,
the old trees die or get taken down.

In some ways, my father's
close, too; we call
a stone by his name.
Now, above his head, the grass blinks,
in spring, when the snow has melted.
Then the lilac blooms, heavy, like clusters of grapes.

They always said
I was like my father, the way he showed
contempt for emotion.
They're the emotional ones,
my sister and my mother.

More and more
my sister comes from the city,
weeds, tidies the garden. My mother
lets her take over: she's the one
who cares, the one who does the work.
To her, it looks like country—
the clipped lawns, strips of colored flowers.
She doesn't know what it once was.

But I know. Like Adam,
I was the firstborn.
Believe me, you never heal,
you never forget the ache in your side,
the place where something was taken away
to make another person.

CHILD CRYING OUT

You're asleep now,
your eyelids quiver.
What son of mine
could be expected
to rest quietly, to live
even one moment
free of wariness?

The night's cold;
you've pushed the covers away.
As for your thoughts, your dreams—

I'll never understand
the claim of a mother
on a child's soul.

So many times
I made that mistake
in love, taking
some wild sound to be
the soul exposing itself—

But not with you,
even when I held you constantly.
You were born, you were far away.

Whatever those cries meant,
they came and went
whether I held you or not,
whether I was there or not.

The soul is silent.
If it speaks at all
it speaks in dreams.

SNOW

Late December: my father and I
are going to New York, to the circus.
He holds me
on his shoulders in the bitter wind:
scraps of white paper
blow over the railroad ties.

My father liked
to stand like this, to hold me
so he couldn't see me.
I remember
staring straight ahead
into the world my father saw;
I was learning
to absorb its emptiness,
the heavy snow
not falling, whirling around us.

TERMINAL RESEMBLANCE

When I saw my father for the last time, we both did the same
    thing.
He was standing in the doorway to the living room,
waiting for me to get off the telephone.
That he wasn't also pointing to his watch
was a signal he wanted to talk.

Talk for us always meant the same thing.
He'd say a few words. I'd say a few back.
That was about it.

It was the end of August, very hot, very humid.
Next door, workmen dumped new gravel on the driveway.

My father and I avoided being alone;
we didn't know how to connect, to make small talk—
there didn't seem to be
any other possibilities.
So this was special: when a man's dying,
he has a subject.

It must have been early morning. Up and down the street
sprinklers started coming on. The gardener's truck
appeared at the end of the block,
then stopped, parking.

My father wanted to tell me what it was like to be dying.
He told me he wasn't suffering.
He said he kept expecting pain, waiting for it, but it never
    came.
All he felt was a kind of weakness.
I said I was glad for him, that I thought he was lucky.

Some of the husbands were getting in their cars, going to
    work.
Not people we knew anymore. New families,
families with young children.
The wives stood on the steps, gesturing or calling.

We said goodbye in the usual way,
no embrace, nothing dramatic.
When the taxi came, my parents watched from the front door,
arm in arm, my mother blowing kisses as she always does,
because it frightens her when a hand isn't being used.
But for a change, my father didn't just stand there.
This time, he waved.

That's what I did, at the door to the taxi.
Like him, waved to disguise my hand's trembling.

LAMENT

Suddenly, after you die, those friends
who never agreed about anything
agree about your character.
They're like a houseful of singers rehearsing
the same score:
you were just, you were kind, you lived a fortunate life.
No harmony. No counterpoint. Except
they're not performers;
real tears are shed.

Luckily, you're dead; otherwise
you'd be overcome with revulsion.
But when that's passed,
when the guests begin filing out, wiping their eyes
because, after a day like this,
shut in with orthodoxy,
the sun's amazingly bright,
though it's late afternoon, September—
when the exodus begins,
that's when you'd feel
pangs of envy.

Your friends the living embrace one another,
gossip a little on the sidewalk
as the sun sinks, and the evening breeze
ruffles the women's shawls—

this, this, is the meaning of
"a fortunate life": it means
to exist in the present.

MIRROR IMAGE

Tonight I saw myself in the dark window as
the image of my father, whose life
was spent like this,
thinking of death, to the exclusion
of other sensual matters,
so in the end that life
was easy to give up, since
it contained nothing: even
my mother's voice couldn't make him
change or turn back
as he believed
that once you can't love another human being
you have no place in the world.

CHILDREN COMING HOME FROM SCHOOL

The year I started school, my sister couldn't walk long
    distances.
Every day, my mother strapped her in the stroller; then,
they'd walk to the corner.
That way, when school was over, I could see them; I could see
    my mother,
first a blur, then a shape with arms.
I walked very slowly, to appear to need nothing.
That's why my sister envied me—she didn't know
you can lie with your face, your body.

She didn't see we were both in false positions.
She wanted freedom. Whereas I continued, in pathetic ways,
to covet the stroller. Meaning
all my life.

And, in that sense, it was lost on me: all the waiting, all my
    mother's
effort to restrain my sister, all the calling, the waving,
since, in that sense, I had no home any longer.

AMAZONS

End of summer: the spruces put out a few green shoots.
Everything else is gold—that's how you know the end of the
    growing season.
A kind of symmetry between what's dying, what's just coming
    to bloom.

It's always been a sensitive time in this family.
We're dying out, too, the whole tribe.
My sister and I, we're the end of something.

Now the windows darken.
And the rain comes, steady and heavy.

In the dining room, the children draw.
That's what we did: when we couldn't see,
we made pictures.

I can see the end: it's the name that's going.
When we're done with it, it's finished, it's a dead language.
That's how language dies, because it doesn't need to be spoken.

My sister and I, we're like amazons,
a tribe without a future.
I watch the children draw: my son, her daughter.
We used soft chalk, the disappearing medium.

CELESTIAL MUSIC

I have a friend who still believes in heaven.
Not a stupid person, yet with all she knows, she literally talks
    to god,
she thinks someone listens in heaven.
On earth, she's unusually competent.
Brave, too, able to face unpleasantness.

We found a caterpillar dying in the dirt, greedy ants crawling
    over it.
I'm always moved by weakness, by disaster, always eager to
    oppose vitality.
But timid, also, quick to shut my eyes.
Whereas my friend was able to watch, to let events play out
according to nature. For my sake, she intervened,
brushing a few ants off the torn thing, and set it down across
    the road.

My friend says I shut my eyes to god, that nothing else
    explains
my aversion to reality. She says I'm like the child who buries
    her head in the pillow
so as not to see, the child who tells herself
that light causes sadness—
My friend is like the mother. Patient, urging me
to wake up an adult like herself, a courageous person—

In my dreams, my friend reproaches me. We're walking
on the same road, except it's winter now;
she's telling me that when you love the world you hear celestial
    music:
look up, she says. When I look up, nothing.
Only clouds, snow, a white business in the trees
like brides leaping to a great height—
Then I'm afraid for her; I see her
caught in a net deliberately cast over the earth—

In reality, we sit by the side of the road, watching the sun set;
from time to time, the silence pierced by a birdcall.
It's this moment we're both trying to explain, the fact
that we're at ease with death, with solitude.
My friend draws a circle in the dirt; inside, the caterpillar
    doesn't move.
She's always trying to make something whole, something
    beautiful, an image
capable of life apart from her.
We're very quiet. It's peaceful sitting here, not speaking, the
    composition
fixed, the road turning suddenly dark, the air
going cool, here and there the rocks shining and glittering—
it's this stillness that we both love.
The love of form is a love of endings.

FIRST MEMORY

Long ago, I was wounded. I lived
to revenge myself
against my father, not
for what he was—
for what I was: from the beginning of time,
in childhood, I thought
that pain meant
I was not loved.
It meant I loved.

A NOTE ABOUT THE AUTHOR

Louise Glück teaches at Williams College and lives in Vermont. She is the author of six books of poems and a collection of essays, entitled *Proofs and Theories*, which won the PEN/Martha Albrand Award. She has been the recipient of the National Book Critics Circle Award for Poetry, the Boston Globe Literary Press Award for Poetry, and the Poetry Society of America's Melville Kane Award and William Carlos Williams Award. She is a Fellow of the American Academy of Arts and Sciences. Her early work has recently been reissued in one volume, *The First Four Books of Poems*. In 1993, she received the Pulitzer Prize for her book *The Wild Iris*.